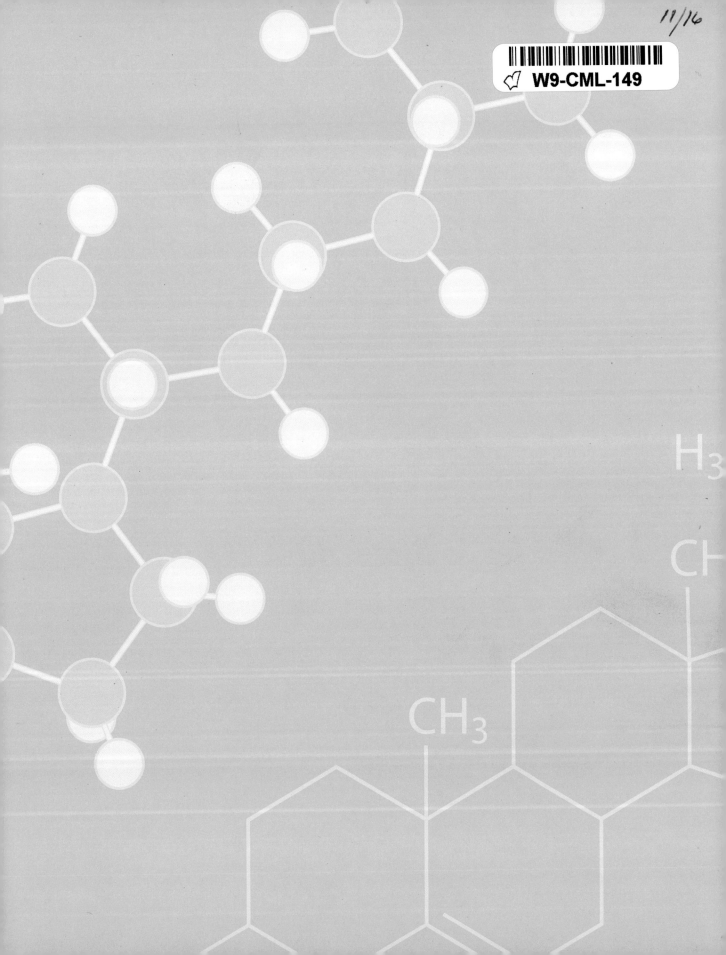

H₃

CH

CH₃

Praise for *The STEM Club Goes Exploring*

"I never knew that there were so many interesting jobs that kids like me could choose from. I really liked how Lois Melbourne had kids explore different career paths while interviewing professionals along the way. When the word "career" comes to mind, I never thought of being able to become a Marine Biologist or an App Programer. Thanks Lois for opening my eyes to an exciting new world of career possibilities!"

—Aiden, Whiz Kid Science

"As a librarian/teacher with over 30 years experience, I am delighted to find The STEM Club Goes Exploring as a resource for students exploring career possibilities in science, technology, engineering and math. Creative in her approach, Lois Melbourne uses a STEM Club field trip to introduce readers to career options that range from game developer to geologist to medical professional."

—Jane Newberry, Librarian at Plano Public Library

"We often hear about the importance of STEM education. In this ground-breaking book, *The STEM Club Goes Exploring*, successful software entrepreneur Lois Melbourne gives life to these words. Through great illustrations, characters and adventures, kids will be engrossed as they learn about the opportunities available through STEM. This book can do more than influence career paths for kids. It can help them understand they can change the world."

—Patrick Hudson, CEO, Robot Entertainment

"Lois Melbourne, former HR Technology CEO and advocate of advancing the future of education, did an outstanding job writing The STEM Club Goes Exploring. As a life-long HR professional, I have seen first-hand how important encouraging children to get involved in STEM coursework can be. I shared the book with my twelve year old boy/ girl twins, and they both responded positively to the messages. It was a great tool for me, as a parent, to start that conversation with my children about the importance of science, engineering, technology and math. Thanks Lois!"

—Trish McFarlane, CEO, Principal Analyst at H3 HR Advisors

"'What I want to be when I grow up' is a question that kids often can't imagine and parents lack the detailed knowledge of careers to truly help guide our kids through the endless choices. In The STEM Club goes Exploring Lois Melbourne breaks down the details of the jobs that make possible all the science and technology that kids already know and use. She not only opens kid's eyes to the many job choices but she also makes these career choices tangible in an animated and easy to read form that will educate without intimidating children. This book is an essential tool not only for the kids that are looking to STEM careers but also to the educators and parents hoping to open their imaginations to all the possibilities."

—Dr. Tina Capps, Veterinarian at Valley Ranch Pet Clinic

Published by Greenleaf Book Group
Austin, Texas
www.gbgpress.com

Distributed by Greenleaf Book Group

For ordering information or special discounts for bulk purchases, please contact Greenleaf Book Group at PO Box 91869, Austin, TX 78709, 512.891.6100.

Design and composition by Greenleaf Book Group
Cover design by Greenleaf Book Group
Illustrations by Jomike Tejido

Cataloging-in-Publication data is available.

Print ISBN: 978-1-62634-303-0
eBook ISBN: 978-1-62634-304-7

Part of the Tree Neutral® program, which offsets the number of trees consumed in the production and printing of this book by taking proactive steps, such as planting trees in direct proportion to the number of trees used: www.treeneutral.com

Manufactured by Oceanic Graphic International on acid-free paper
Manufactured in Guang Dong, China on April 25, 2016
Batch No. TT16010649

16 17 18 19 20 21   10 9 8 7 6 5 4 3 2 1

First Edition

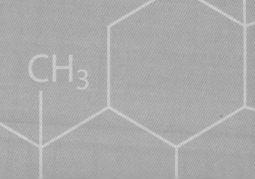

The STEM CLUB GOES EXPLORING

MY FUTURE STORY

LOIS MELBOURNE

Illustrated by JOMIKE TEJIDO

This is just one book in the series about exploring
careers by Lois Melbourne of My Future Story, who wants
to inspire readers to find their passion and use it to
explore and shape their own future stories.

GREENLEAF
BOOK GROUP PRESS

The STEM Club

Sara   Jenny   Fran   Nixie

Betik Jesse Patti Winston

" **H**i! I'm Fran. Everyone in school is really excited about Favorites Day, the day when each of us presents a favorite career and shows off why we think it's great! This year, the STEM Club is creating a video showcasing careers in Science, Technology, Engineering, and Math (that's what STEM stands for!). You might be surprised at the wide variety of cool jobs that we're investigating.

"This project is perfect for me because I want to be a science and technology reporter in the future—so I'll practice my writing and reporting skills! I'm also producing the STEM Club video. Today, we'll interview different people based on our favorite interests."

"**M**r. Day is our STEM Club sponsor at school. He has asked us what jobs we'd like to explore in science, technology, engineering, and math. Now he's taking us on field trips to different workplaces in our community.

"First, we're going to a video game company, which was Nixie's choice. Some STEM jobs work inside and some are mostly done outside. Betik knows he wants to work outside—not spend all day in an office. By the time this project is done, we will have visited labs, factories, offices, a mine, a farm and a hospital. Each location includes STEM careers."

"Nixie is excited to do an on-camera interview with her uncle, an entrepreneur who started his own company! She's going to ask questions about the jobs people do to create apps."

"**U**ncle Ross," Nixie says, "I love the apps I play with everyday, but I don't know what jobs it takes to make them. Are all of the people working here programmers writing the software?"

"It takes many different jobs to create an app," Uncle Ross responds. "First, product managers research what software people will buy. They decide what the software will actually do. They also manage the business side by calculating how much it will cost to build the software. Then they identify which additional employees will be needed to get the job done, like the graphic designers who draw the characters and their worlds."

"Do the programmers build the app next, Uncle Ross?"

"No, then product designers figure out how the software will work and what it will look like," Uncle Ross responds. "They plan things like what will happen when you click on the robot in a game, or what pops up to show you how many coins you've earned. Graphic designers help the product designers by creating the buttons, characters, and pictures for the screen."

"I bet then it's time for the programmers to work their magic!"

"Right you are, Nixie!" Uncle Ross says. "Now the programmers create the code that really makes the app work. Building software is a real team effort."

"What is this team doing, Uncle Ross?"

"They are quality testers who use the software just like you and your friends use it. They evaluate it by playing the game. Then they share with the developers any problems or ideas they have to make it better. Sometimes the team finds a bug or a glitch in the software."

"I bet it's a bummer if something doesn't work right," Nixie says.

"That's why the tester's job is so important," Uncle Ross responds. "The programmers fix the problem, and then the software goes back to the testers again to make sure it's working right."

"Thanks so much for taking the time to give us a tour and explaining these fabulous jobs, Uncle Ross!"

"So, do any of these jobs sound good to you?" he asks.

Nixie says, "I don't think I'll ever look at my apps the same way again! I think the product designer job sounds the best. I like the idea of pulling everything together and being creative. It sounds a little like being the director of a movie."

"These are just the technology jobs involved in building software," Uncle Ross replies. "Maybe the next time you visit, we can talk about other jobs in the company that involve accounting, advertising, and selling the software. They are the 'behind the scenes' jobs that help to make a company run well and be successful."

"Okay, everyone! Our next stop is the vet's office," Fran says. "Winston's cousin Bobby is working there while going to veterinary school."

Mr. Day asks, "While we're on our way, can anyone think of jobs that might've been involved in creating this GPS?"

Winston jumps in, "The Global Positioning System has software, so I bet it needed all of those jobs we saw at the software company."

"Oh, I LOVE GPS maps!" Sara says. "Can you imagine the math involved in getting the distances right—and the technology it takes to track different vehicle locations for the traffic map systems on our phones and in our cars? Math is so important. Did you know that most people use it every day without even thinking about it? But I think about math ALL the time."

Mr. Day smiles, "I bet someday you'll have a job that involves math because you like it so much, Sara."

"I'm picturing all of the jobs involved in building the satellites that circle the earth and the receiving devices, like the GPS," Winston adds. "Just look at all of the cool gadgets right here in Mr. Day's van. They were all dreamed up and designed by somebody!"

inston begins, "Bobby, thanks for talking to us about veterinary school. You work part-time in the vet's office helping animals while you go to school. What are your plans when you graduate?"

"Glad to chat with you Winston!" Bobby smiles, "Officially, I'm studying veterinary medicine, but I'm not going to be a vet when I graduate. I made a list of the jobs my classmates and I are doing now or are considering doing after we graduate. We're all getting the same veterinary degree but we'll be applying for different jobs in a few years."

"All of these jobs help animals in some way. Which job do you want?" Winston asks.

"I love animals and enjoy working

Jobs Helping Animals:
- Animal medicine researcher
- Animal behaviorist
- Animal trainer
- Dog food maker
- Humane Society director
- Pet groomer
- Pet rescuer
- Veterinarian
- Wildlife rehabilitator
- Zoo keeper
- Zoologist

with them here at the office. But I also really love chemistry and research. So I'm going to be an animal medicine researcher! I'll design different medicines and vitamins to help the animals stay healthy."

Winston asks, "What happens if you change your mind about what you want to do?"

"You can change what you study,"

Bobby replies. "It might take a little longer to graduate, because some jobs need more specific classes than others. But that's OK. It's important to learn about your career options while you're in school."

"I think rescued pets are the best," Winston says. "The people that work to save and find homes for animals are totally AWESOME!"

"What other jobs are available after you and your friends graduate from vet school, Bobby?"

"Well, my friend loves to cook! She wants to make pet food like you buy at the store. This degree helps her understand the nutrition needs of animals. There are many jobs that focus on the health and training of animals. So, Winston, let me ask you a question: Do you want to work with animals, too?"

"Absolutely! I want to study whales, dolphins, and fish. I'd like to study at a Florida college. The schools there are close to the water so I can observe marine life in its natural habitat. What would my degree be called if I studied marine animals, Bobby?"

"It's called *marine biology* and that's a great idea, Winston! There are many ocean creatures to take care of—all over the world. Did you know that approximately 71 percent of Earth's surface is water? And we've explored less than 5 percent of the oceans!"

"Now that's what I call a lot of water and sea creatures to study!"

"OK, folks," Fran claps her hands, "we have to keep on schedule. Let's get moving!"

"Thanks for organizing everything and keeping us on track, Fran. I'm really excited to visit the mine," Betik says. "You know my motto: Rocks ROCK!"

"James is usually the one keeping us on track," Winston says. "It's too bad he's sick today. He loves his computer's calendar and organizing everything we do, doesn't he, Sara?"

"He sure does," Sara responds. "The coolest jobs I've found that keep track of scheduling are at the airport. Think about all the scheduling that has to be done; flights, passenger check-in, baggage loading, and all those employees!"

"Betik, what do you call the guys who sit in the big tower at the airport?" Sara asks.

"They're called *air traffic controllers*. They have to
schedule in real-time, meaning they make decisions on
the spot about what is happening with all of the take-offs
and landings. I bet James would like to work at the airport
someday. He gets so excited when he talks about it."

"I'm so glad Mr. Day introduced us to you, Mr. Reed," Betik exclaims. "It's really cool that you guys went to college together! Can you tell me why a geology scientist is needed at a mine?"

"Great question, Betik! My team and I are responsible for researching and finding the best pieces of land for a mining company to buy, and where the workers will dig for copper and other metals. My geology degree taught me how to do this."

"Do you travel much, Mr. Reed?"

"I travel all over the world," Mr. Reed says. I visit existing mines and also test soil and study the land and rocks of new places that companies want to mine. I'm interested in what Earth is made of and how it was formed. My brother is a geologist, too! He works for an oil company and travels around the world seeking new places to find oil. He also studies existing oil fields and makes sure the environment is protected around them."

"If I decide to become a geologist, what courses should I take in college?" Betik asks.

"You'll need to mostly study minerals, chemistry, and geography."

"**W**hat other kinds of jobs can you do with a geology degree, Mr. Reed?"

"Some geologists study volcanoes, earthquakes, ancient building sites, and archaeology."

"But why do we need geologists to study Earth? Why is the information they gather so important?" Betik asks.

"Geology scientists help solve problems, such as the causes of natural disasters and climate change. They also help to manage the resources we dig out from Earth for energy consumption and manufacturing," Mr. Reed explains.

"The geologist who took the coolest trip was Astronaut Jack Schmitt. In 1972, he was a member of the Apollo 17 space mission. He walked on the moon, exploring and gathering soil samples and lunar rocks to bring home and study.

"Did you know that there's currently a shortage of well-trained geologists? Betik, are you interested in this field of work?"

"I sure am—especially after you've shared the important work geologists do. Thank you, Mr. Reed! Rocks ROCK!" Betik shakes Mr. Reed's hand in gratitude.

"Look, there's an electric car!" Fran says. "It doesn't need gas. It's so cool that after all the years that cars have worked one way, there's now a completely different way to make cars: No gasoline—just batteries!"

"Electric cars are much better for the environment," Winston adds.

Patti says, "That car is proof that creativity is needed in STEM careers, too, Winston. It seems like most STEM careers are about solving problems in new ways."

"I believe in creativity! That's why I doodle on everything," Winston says, "even my math homework. Research says that doodling helps you think better."

"Ooooh," Mr. Day says teasingly, "so that's why you draw on everything you turn in!"

"Problem solving is all about creativity, Mr. Day," Winston responds. "Don't you want to help people solve their health problems, Patti?"

"You're right. I'm a little nervous about my interview at the hospital, but I've practiced a lot and Dr. Carlton is very important to me."

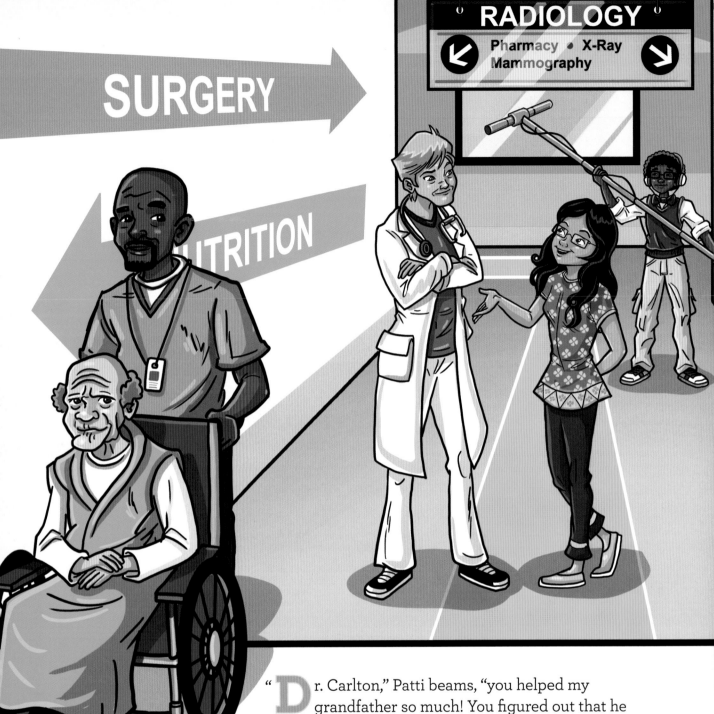

"Dr. Carlton," Patti beams, "you helped my grandfather so much! You figured out that he didn't feel well because he had a heart attack. And you're the reason why he feels good today! Can you tell me how you did that?"

"Actually, it wasn't just *ME* that helped your grandfather, Patti. Who was the person who helped him begin to make healthy food choices?"

"Oh, right, the nutritionist!" Patti responds. "Grandpa and I met with her. She's trained to help people adjust their eating habits so that they don't get sick again."

"That's right, Patti! There are **so** many people responsible for helping patients heal. Most people know a little about what nurses and doctors do each day. But did you know there are many, many types of doctors who practice more than 100 specialties? There are also jobs that focus on research, creating medicines, selling medical supplies, and processing medical data. Although some of these workers may never meet the people they help, they are **very** important."

"**G**randpa needed help getting exercise, too."

"That's right!" the doctor agreed. "Physical therapists are special kinds of trainers that need to know about illnesses, injuries, and how to help people recover using physical training. You can see there are many people on your grandfather's health team. Are you considering a job in medicine, Patti?"

"I'm exploring jobs that help people stay healthy or help to heal them. But I don't think I want to go to medical school," Patti responds. "But, X-rays and the equipment used in hospitals fascinate me!"

"I'm so happy that you want to help, Patti! There are many ways to work in the health care industry without going to medical school. Workers with specialized training are needed to help care for people who have a wide variety of health needs. There's an entire industry dedicated to making the specialized equipment used in hospitals."

" **I**t's time to get back to school. I hope the rest of the stoplights are green the whole way! I don't want to be late," Fran says.

"That reminds me," Jesse replied. "Did you see my interview with my neighbor who works for the city?"

"Not yet. What's it about, Jesse?"

"My neighbor studies the traffic flow in the city and uses math and computer programs to set up how long each street light is green, yellow, and red. She keeps the traffic moving according to where the most cars are coming and going. She works with other civil engineers who plan buildings, bridges, parks, water supply systems, and all the things that make up the physical parts of cities. She called it *infrastructure*. That's the kind of engineering I want to study!"

"Wow," Fran says, "that sounds like a real challenge!"

"**W**e have a video in our presentation that shows lots of things that mechanical engineers design—like cameras, cars, and cranes," Jesse says.

"Jesse, how do you know so much about the jobs at the factory we visited last week?"

"I went on the Internet and did a Google search. I typed in: 'Who designs machines for factories?'"

"What did you find?" Fran asks.

"I found out that mechanical engineers are responsible for designing machines. Machines have always interested me. My class once went on a field trip to a factory. We saw huge machines—in action—that baked, sliced, and packaged bread. A mechanical engineer designed all of those machines."

"During our research," Jenny says, "Jesse and I discovered that mechanical engineers design tools and machines. Sometimes mechanical engineers are described as *movement engineers*, because they design anything that needs to move."

"Tell me about your presentation, Jenny," Fran prompts.

"During my research, I discovered that website with the monster on it. It showed all kinds of engineering jobs! Engineers are the ones that figure out ways to solve problems with science *and* math. I **love** that!"

"So, Jenny and I decided that our presentation should focus on different kinds of engineers," Jesse says.

"What kinds?" Fran asks.

"Chemical engineers use chemicals to transform other materials," Jesse responds. "They create things like paint that won't release fumes or fabrics that won't wrinkle. They even create fire resistant clothing—like the turnout gear firefighters wear."

"Wow," Fran says, "that's amazing!"

"Molecular engineers work with machines that are so small you can't see them with your eye," Jenny continues. "They call it *nanotechnology*."

"And," Jesse concludes, "electrical engineers design and build technology that involves electricity—like electric motors, solar power equipment, and high-tech medical tools."

"Now that we've finished filming our interviews, Betik, we're ready to edit them together."

"Should we start with the footage from the organic farm? We need to show the computers in the tractor. It is **so** much more high tech than I expected!"

"That's a great idea! Let's be sure to also include the math jobs."

"In the math section, I've included the accountant that manages the money for your dad's company, Fran. I've also included the architect, the construction worker, and the city planner."

"Good thinking, Betik! I can't wait to share our video during Favorites Day! The variety of career options that we have explored is amazing! Even though we all go to the same school now, we will grow up to have very different jobs in many different places! One of the biggest lessons I've learned from making our video is that I can plan my career to include the things I like best! And so can you!"

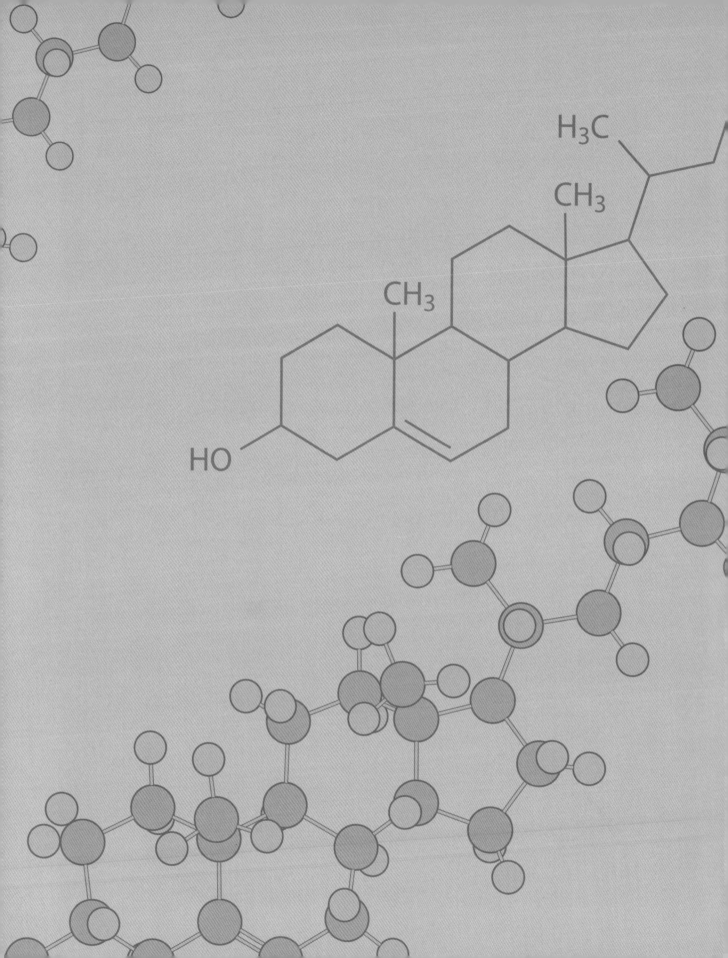

Glossary of Careers

Air Traffic Controller: An airline worker who safely directs aircraft on the ground and through airspace, by receiving and processing data from radar and other devices that monitor local weather conditions, and by maintaining radio contact with pilots. This job takes a lot of concentration and a calm attitude.

Animal Behaviorist: A scientist who studies the ways in which animals interact with each other, the environment, and people. A behaviorist can work indoors and/or outdoors, depending on the animals and the location of where the animals need to be studied.

Animal Trainer: A person who teaches animals (and sometimes their owners) how to act and react using commands. Sometimes the training is designed to create entertainment. Other times the training is to promote good behavior.

Animal Medicine Researcher: A person who conducts an organized investigation of medicines to be taken by animals, and then designs new medicines and vitamins. A researcher may also evaluate a medicine's effectiveness and safeness for animals.

Chemical Engineer

Chemical Engineer: An engineer who is responsible for chemical production and the manufacture of products through chemical processes. This job requires very specific and specialized science classes to prepare someone for the work.

City Planner: A person who helps a community decide how to best use its land and resources, and then draws an organized arrangement of streets, parks, businesses, and residential areas. The bigger the city, the more complex the planning. Many big cities have teams of planners that work together to understand all aspects of what a city needs and requires.

Geologist/Geology Scientist

Civil Engineer: An engineer who designs and maintains public works, including roads, bridges, dams, and other structures. A civil engineer often works with city planners, architects, and environmental experts to make these big projects possible.

Electrical Engineer: An engineer who deals with the technology of electricity, especially the design and application of circuitry and equipment for power generation. This job involves a lot of computer work and a person is required to take specialized classes.

Geologist/Geology Scientist: A scientist who studies what Earth is made of and how it was formed. This job is needed by many companies throughout the world, especially when a company is dependent on using Earth's materials or resources to do business.

Graphic Designer: A person who uses the elements of art to communicate a business message. A graphic designer's work is seen every day in the different kinds of ads found in magazines, online, and so on. This job relies on computer technology.

Graphic Designer

Pet Groomer: A person who bathes, brushes, trims, and provides other grooming services for pets, such as cats and dogs. A groomer can also be part of a pet's healthcare team, identifying potential health issues, such as tooth decay and ear infections.

Humane Society Director: A person who oversees a group of people whose aim is to stop animal suffering due to cruelty or other reasons. This job is very important in helping animals find homes. The director is often responsible for finding new ways to educate people about how rescued animals can make great pets.

Marine Biologist: A scientist who studies organisms found in oceans or other marine bodies of water. In order to qualify for this popular job, many specialized higher education classes are required.

Marine Biologist

Mechanical Engineer: An engineer who uses the principles of engineering, physics, and materials science to design, produce, and maintain tools, machinery, and other products. Nearly everything that has moving parts, found at home and in school, was designed by a mechanical engineer.

Molecular Engineer: An engineer who manufactures molecules or creates new manufacturing materials using them. A molecular engineer works with things so small that you cannot see them without a microscope or other tool that magnifies their image.

Nutritionist: A person who advises others on aspects of food and diet that impact their health.

Physical Therapist: A licensed health care professional who helps patients reduce pain and improve or restore mobility after a surgery or an illness. This job is a good example of a medical job that does not require going to medical school. However, it does require specific education and training.

Product Manager: A person who is responsible for analyzing market conditions and defining features or functions of a product or product family.

Programmer: A person who writes computer programs.

Programmer

Quality Tester: A person who tests computer programs or apps to ensure they are working properly.

Software Product Designer: A person who creates a new program or improves existing applications (also called "apps") to be sold by a business to its customers, by generating and developing new ideas. This technical job is also creative. The look and function of an app is a huge factor in determining its success.

Veterinarian: A doctor who is trained to give medical care and treatment to animals.

Veterinarian

Wildlife Rehabilitator: A person who cares for and treats injured, orphaned, or sick wild animals so that they can be released back into the wild or returned to their homes.

Zookeeper: A person who maintains or cares for animals in a zoo.

Zoologist: A scientist who studies animals and their behaviors. Despite the word zoo in the name, this job is not related to the zoo.

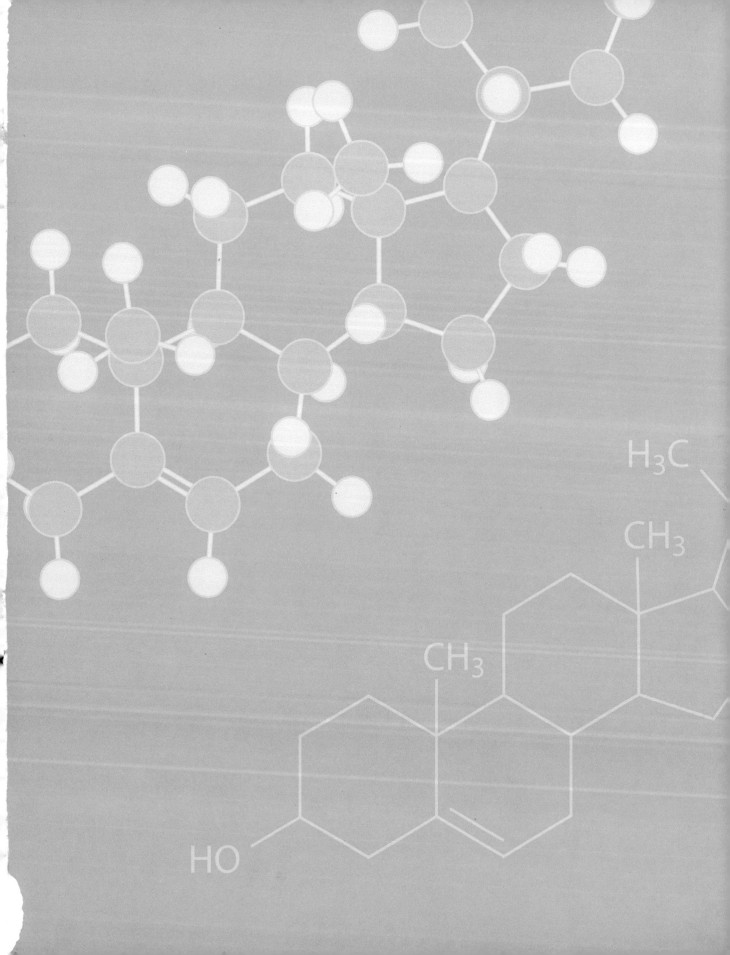

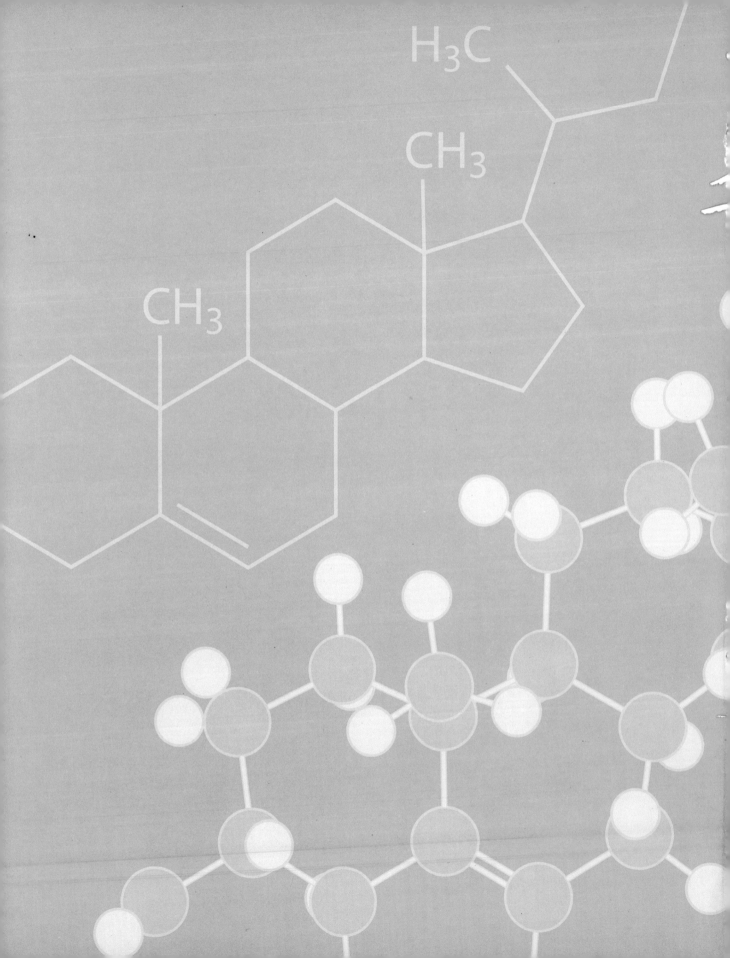